Graphic Sparks are published by Stone Arch Books,
151 Good Counsel Drive, P.O. Box 669,
Mankato, Minnesota 56002.
www.stonearchbooks.com

Library of Congress Cataloging-in-Publication Data
Nickel, Scott.
    Curse of the Red Scorpion / by Scott Nickel; illustrated by Steve Harpster.
    p. cm. — (Graphic Sparks)
    ISBN-13: 978-1-59889-034-1 (hardcover)
    ISBN-10: 1-59889-034-4 (hardcover)
    ISBN-13: 978-1-59889-169-0 (paperback)
    ISBN-10: 1-59889-169-3 (paperback)
    1. Graphic novels. I. Harpster, Steve. II. Title. III. Series.
PN6727.N544C87 2006
741.5—dc22   2005026684

Summary: Mitchell was bored at the museum — until he saw the amazing Red Scorpion
of Manzitopia! Now he thinks the creature has followed him home. Do claws click in the
night? Does a stinger hide in the curtains? Will Mitchell trap the beast before he becomes
its next victim?

Art Director: Heather Kindseth
Production Manager: Sharon Reid
Production/Design: James Liebman, Mie Tsuchida
Production Assistance: Bob Horvath, Eric Murray

CURSE OF THE RED SCORPION

BY SCOTT NICKEL

ILLUSTRATED BY STEVE HARPSTER

STONE ARCH BOOKS
Minneapolis   San Diego

CAST OF CHARACTERS

MOTHER

RED SCORPION

MITCHELL'S CAT

FATHER

**MUSEUM
ATTENDANT**

**MITCHELL
MARTIN**

5

22

23

ABOUT THE AUTHOR

Scott Nickel has written children's books, short fiction for *Boys' Life Magazine*, humorous greeting cards, and lots of really funny knock-knock jokes. Scott is also the author of many Garfield books.

Currently, Scott lives in Indiana with his wife, two sons, four cats, a parakeet, and several sea monkeys.

ABOUT THE ILLUSTRATOR

Steve Harpster has loved to draw funny cartoons, mean monsters, and goofy gadgets since he was able to pick up a pencil. In first grade, he was able to avoid his writing assignments by working on the pictures for stories instead.

Steve was able to land a job drawing funny pictures for books, and that's really what he's best at. Steve lives in Columbus, Ohio, with his wonderful wife, Karen, and their sheepdog, Doodle.

GLOSSARY

curse (KURSS) a spell intended to harm someone, so having a younger sister or brother really isn't a curse even though it may seem like one

legend (LEJ-uhnd) a story that has been around for a long time; legends may or may not be true.

Manzitopia (man-zuh-TOH-pee-uh) a make-believe place where the Red Scorpion used to live

rock man (ROK MAN) any guy weird enough to love rocks

specimen (SPESS-uh-muhn) a sample of a larger group of things; a zoo might have specimens of deadly creatures for people to see and study safely.

Super Soak Water Blaster (SOO-pur SOHK WAW-tur BLAST-ur) the ultimate weapon for fighting off nighttime intruders

Some of these word specimens are hundreds of years old!

STINGING SCORPION SMARTS

Scorpions can have as many as 12 eyes.

The most common pet scorpion is the Emperor Scorpion. Its sting is like that of a wasp or bee. It can grow to a length of 6 inches.

Scorpions are nocturnal. This means they only move around at night, but not in people's dreams.

There are over 1500 species of scorpions, but only about 20-25 of them are dangerous to people.

Scorpions have been around for 400 million years.

When a scorpion is threatened, it will lift its tail above its head. This makes it look even scarier, and then the predator will usually leave it alone.

DISCUSSION QUESTIONS

1.) Mitchell keeps seeing the dreaded Red
   Scorpion in his room. But every time
   he turns on the lights, it turns out to be
   something else. Have you ever thought
   you saw something in your room that
   wasn't really there?

2.) What would you do if you were Mitchell
   and you kept dreaming about the Red
   Scorpion?

3.) The museum guide knows a lot about
   amazing rocks and minerals, such as the
   ruby eyes of the Red Scorpion. Do you
   think he knows more about the scorpion
   than he tells the kids? Do you think he has
   had his own strange encounter with the
   creature? Why or why not?

WRITING PROMPTS

1.) Mitchell creates an amazing trap to catch the scorpion. Think about the different objects in your own room and build a trap with them. Describe your trap in detail and don't forget to tell us what you're going to catch.

2.) Oh no, you just went to the Museum of Natural History! While you were there you saw something you will never forget. Was it a dinosaur? Was it a mummy? Describe what you saw and why it scared you.

3.) We've all had bad dreams before. Write about your scariest dream and how you got over it.

INTERNET

Do you want to know more about subjects related to this book? Or are you interested in learning about other topics? Then check out FactHound, a fun, easy way to find Internet sites.

Our investigative staff has already sniffed out great sites for you!

Here's how to use FactHound:

1.) Visit www.facthound.com

2.) Select your grade level.

3.) To learn more about subjects related to this book, type in the book's ISBN number: 1598890344. If you're looking for information on another subject, simply type in a keyword.

4.) Click the *Fetch It* button.

FactHound will fetch the best Internet sites for you.

www.FactHound.com
SM